BALLPARK Mysteries 4

THE ASTRO
OUTLAW

THE ASTRO
OUTLAW

by David A. Kelly
illustrated by Mark Meyers

A STEPPING STONE BOOK™
Random House 🏠 New York

To Adam from Colorado, Anya from Massachusetts, Sam from
Wisconsin, Isaac from Washington, D.C., and all the other kids who've
discovered the joys of reading through the Ballpark Mysteries —D.A.K.

To Bob and Kay. You guys rock! —M.M.

*"People ask me what I do in winter when there's no baseball. I'll tell you
what I do. I stare out the window and wait for spring."*
—Rogers Hornsby, Hall of Fame infielder and Texas native

Text copyright © 2012 by David A. Kelly
Cover art and interior illustrations copyright © 2012 by Mark Meyers

Published in the United States by Random House Children's Books, a division of Random
House, Inc., New York.

Random House and the colophon are registered trademarks and A Stepping Stone Book
and the colophon are trademarks of Random House, Inc.

Visit us on the Web!
SteppingStonesBooks.com
www.randomhouse.com/kids

Educators and librarians, for a variety of teaching tools, visit us at
www.randomhouse.com/teachers

Library of Congress Cataloging-in-Publication Data
Kelly, David A. (David Andrew)
The Astro outlaw / by David A. Kelly ; illustrated by Mark Meyers.
p. cm. — (Ballpark mysteries ; #4) ("A stepping stone book.")
Summary: While visiting Houston, Texas, Mike and Kate tour the Johnson Space Center
with an astronaut in the morning and at the Houston Astros' ball game that evening,
the cousins search for the person who steals the astronaut's moon rock when he arrives
at the stadium to sign autographs.
ISBN 978-0-375-86883-2 (pbk.) — ISBN 978-0-375-96883-9 (lib. bdg.) —
ISBN 978-0-375-89966-9 (ebook)
[1. Baseball—Fiction. 2. Cousins—Fiction. 3. Houston (Tex.)—Fiction. 4. Mystery and
detective stories.] I. Meyers, Mark, ill. II. Title.
PZ7.K2936Ast 2012 [Fic]—dc22 2011013999

Printed in the United States of America
10 9 8 7 6 5 4 3 2 1

Contents

Houston, We Have a Problem

Mike Walsh stared out of a big white space helmet. His breathing echoed in his ears. He saw a spacecraft from the corner of his eye. It felt like he was walking on the moon.

Mike tried to lift up the helmet's shiny gold visor so he could see better. But the thick rubbery astronaut gloves he wore made it hard. His fingers fumbled with the helmet.

"Houston, we have a problem!" Mike said to his cousin Kate Hopkins. "I'm trapped!"

It was spring break. Kate, Mike, and Kate's dad were taking a VIP tour of NASA's Johnson Space Center in Houston, Texas. They were in town to visit Mr. Ryan, a friend of Kate's dad. Like Mr. Hopkins, Mr. Ryan was a baseball scout. He worked for the Houston Astros and had given them free tickets for the tour and the Astros game that night.

Kate laughed. "The only problem Houston has is *you*!" she said, shaking her head. Mike was always fooling around. Kate flipped up the gold visor on his helmet. "Commander Rice told us how to open the visor earlier."

"Can't hear you," Mike joked. "We're on the moon, remember? Sound waves can't travel because there's no air in space."

Kate rolled her eyes and turned to watch Commander Rice, the tall, athletic astronaut leading the tour. Other than Kate, Mike, and

Mr. Hopkins, the rest of the people on the tour were local business owners. Kate and Mike had met Sam Shine, a used-car dealer, Tex Rayburn, who owned a hat store called Fat Hats, and Manuel Lopez, an insurance salesman. The group was in a large training room filled with spacecraft replicas. Commander Rice was showing them how astronauts lived and worked in space. He picked up a chunk of black rock and held it out to the group.

"Is that a moon rock?" Tex Rayburn asked. He wore black cowboy boots and a black cowboy hat. His big brass belt buckle spelled out FAT HATS.

Commander Rice shook his head. "No, it's just a model we use for training," he told Tex. "Maybe I can show you a real one later. They're very valuable."

"Shoot. You can put your boots in the

oven, but that don't make 'em biscuits," Tex said. "I reckon we can wait a little to see a *real* moon rock."

Commander Rice put the rock down on a nearby table. Then he explained how astronauts take showers in space. Or how they don't. In space, regular showers won't work. Without gravity, water doesn't fall to the ground. Instead, astronauts use damp towels to wash up.

"Where do y'all get the water from?" Sam asked.

"We bring water with us," Commander Rice said. "Or we recycle it from the air and the water we use every day. We even have to recycle toilet water. Anyone want a sip?"

"YUCK!" Kate said, making a face.

Most of the members of the tour shook their heads. "No thank you," Tex said. "I always drink upstream from the herd."

Commander Rice laughed. "The filters make our water cleaner than any creek." He checked his watch. "I still have time to show you the mission control room."

Kate rapped Mike's helmet with her knuckles. "Hey, take that off. We're going to see mission control!"

Mike removed the helmet and placed it on a table. Tex slapped him on the back.

"Son, that helmet's too hot for Houston. Stop by my store, Fat Hats!" Tex boomed. He handed Mike a business card. It had a picture of a ten-gallon hat on it. "We'll fix y'all up with a proper Texas hat."

Tex winked at Mike and followed Commander Rice through the door. Mike and Kate rushed to catch up. The commander led them to a building across the street.

After passing through security, they went

up a flight of stairs and through a heavy door. To their side stood four long rows of metal desks, filled with old-fashioned computers. Five large screens hung on the wall at the front of the room. Pictures of the moon, the earth, and a map of the world played across them.

"Welcome to NASA's mission control," Commander Rice said. "It's the exact one that

was used for the Apollo moon missions. Have a seat."

Mike and Kate scrambled for one of the desk chairs. Mr. Hopkins and some of the other visitors stood against the wall.

"Mission control is where flight controllers keep an eye on spacecraft and astronauts after they lift off into space," Commander Rice said. He explained how different people were in charge of different parts of a spaceflight. For example, a controller in the first row managed the spacecraft's direction. A controller in the second row kept track of the crew's health.

Commander Rice also told them about the Apollo rockets that traveled from the earth to the moon and back between 1968 and 1972.

Mike raised his hand. "Is that how we got the moon rocks?"

Commander Rice nodded and pushed some buttons at one of the desks. A picture of an astronaut flashed up on one of the screens. He was standing on the moon, holding a moon rock.

"On six missions, the Apollo astronauts brought back over eight hundred pounds of rocks," Commander Rice told them. "Some were black. Others were white. And some were shades of gray."

"Can we see one?" Tex called out.

Commander Rice checked his watch. "We're out of time. Come to tonight's game," he said with a grin. "I'll be signing autographs near the main entrance. I'll also have a moon rock on display." He led the group down the stairs and back to their bus.

"I hope to see you two at the game tonight," Commander Rice said to Kate and Mike as they boarded the bus. "Mr. Ryan said you were extra-special guests."

Mike gave him a thumbs-up and went to sit with Kate a few rows from the back. Mr. Hopkins sat in front of them. As the bus started up, he leaned over the top of his seat. "How'd you like that tour?" he asked. "I remember seeing mission control on television when I was younger."

"It was great!" Mike said. "But I was

hoping we'd get to eat freeze-dried space food. Or some of that space dots ice cream."

"Real astronauts don't eat space dots!" Kate piped up. She pointed to a page in the space book she had bought at the gift shop. It was filled with pictures of space food. "They don't have ice cream in space. They don't even have refrigerators or freezers. And guess what—NO pizza!"

"No ice cream? No pizza?" Mike yelped. "If I were an astronaut, I'd starve!"

"You won't starve tonight," Kate's dad said. "We're going out to dinner before the game with Mr. Ryan. Barbecue was our favorite when we worked together for the Dodgers."

Kate's father was a scout for the L.A. Dodgers. Kate didn't see him very often because her parents were divorced. He lived in Los Angeles, and she lived with her mother in Cooperstown, New York. Mike's house was just down the street from hers. His parents owned a sporting goods store in town.

The rest of the way back, Mike and Kate took turns pretending to be astronauts and controllers at mission control. Mr. Hopkins flipped through Kate's space book.

That evening, Mike, Kate, and Mr. Hopkins met Mr. Ryan for dinner at Deano's Bar-B-Que. Mr. Ryan was short and stocky, with frizzy black hair. He looked more like a wrestler than a baseball scout. But he sure knew a lot of baseball stories. While they waited for their food, Mr. Ryan told Mike and Kate secrets about their favorite players.

After dinner, they walked over to the stadium. Mr. Ryan had reserved seats right behind the Astros' dugout. When they sat down, Mr. Ryan pointed out the ballpark's movable roof. It was wide open. Lights from the city of Houston sparkled against the darkening sky.

"It gets very hot here in Texas. We have one of the few stadiums with a roof that opens and closes," Mr. Ryan said. "You get such a nice view of the city when the roof is open." He folded his arms across his chest and leaned back in his chair to admire Houston's skyline.

"Hey, Mr. Ryan," Mike broke in, "why is there a train up there?" He pointed to a huge black steam engine and coal car on top of the ballpark's left-field wall. The train had big red wheels, a bright red cowcatcher, a headlight, and a large black smokestack.

"Trains are an important part of Houston's history," Mr. Ryan said. "And the Astros' ballpark was built on the site of the old train yards. The whistle blows at the start of each game and for every Astros home run and win."

While they waited for the game to start, Mike tossed his baseball in the air. He always tried to bring one to games. Kate read through the program her dad had bought.

The announcer's voice boomed over the loudspeaker. "Please give a big round of applause for our special guest tonight, NASA Commander Nicholas Rice! After throwing out the game's first pitch, he'll be signing autographs near the main entrance. Stop by and you'll also be able to see a real, priceless moon rock!"

The crowd stood up and cheered. Everyone waited for Commander Rice to run out to the pitcher's mound. The Houston Astros catcher crouched behind home plate. After a few minutes, he stood up. He looked from one side to the other like he had lost something. Both teams milled around by their dugouts.

Kate tugged on her father's shirt. "Shouldn't Commander Rice be coming out?" she asked.

Kate's dad scanned the stadium. "Maybe he's still getting ready," he said.

Again, the announcer came over the loudspeaker. "Please give a big Texas welcome to our special guest, Commander Rice!"

The crowd cheered. The catcher returned to his crouch. The teams watched from the sidelines. But no astronaut came onto the field. The umpires huddled at first base. Several of them pointed to the clock on the scoreboard.

The loudspeaker crackled one more time. "Houston, we have a problem," the voice said. "Our astronaut is missing!"

Lost in Space

"Missing? Commander Rice is missing?" Mike asked. "What happened? Maybe he's been kidnapped!"

"I doubt it," Kate's dad said. He raised his eyebrows at Mr. Ryan. "He's probably just caught in traffic or something. Anyway, why would anyone want to kidnap him?"

"Because he's got a valuable moon rock with him!" Mike said. "It's a lot easier to steal a moon rock than to go to the moon yourself!"

"Shh," Kate said. "Something's happening."

Out on the field, the head umpire jogged over to the Astros' dugout. He talked to the manager. A minute later, the Astros ran onto the field. As they did, the steam train on the left-field wall chugged along the tracks. It blew its whistle. *WOOOO-WOOOO!* The train engineer waved to the crowd.

Mr. Hopkins relaxed. He put one arm around Kate. With the other he made notes about the ballpark in his notebook.

"Always working, eh, Dad?" Kate said. "Or are you writing down ideas for my birthday? You know, I'd like a new camera so I can take better pictures for Mike's website." Mike wrote about ballparks and baseball on his website, dugoutscoop.com. Sometimes Kate helped.

Mr. Hopkins smiled and slipped the notebook back in his pocket. "I'll keep that in mind," he said. "But I'm afraid you're never short of birthday ideas."

"Looks like the game is going to start. Make some noise!" Mr. Ryan said. Kate and Mike clapped with the other fans. Mr. Ryan rolled up his program and thumped it loudly against his palm. "Come on, TOMMY!" he bellowed. "Tommy Thompson is our best pitcher. We can't lose with him on the mound!"

Thompson didn't let Mr. Ryan down. He struck out the first three Colorado Rockies in a row.

Mr. Ryan thumped his program against his palm again. *THWWWAPP!* "What'd I tell you?" he said to Mike as the teams switched sides. "Tommy's great."

Houston came to bat and quickly got two men on base. Then the Astros' star hitter, Adam Bixby, strolled up to home plate.

"He's a great hitter, but watch his stance," Mr. Hopkins said. "He keeps his feet close together."

"I hope he hits a home run," said Mike.

Bixby waited patiently while three balls went by. Usually with three balls and no strikes, batters don't swing at the next pitch. They know if it's a ball, they'll earn a trip to first base. But Bixby didn't let the pitch go by. His heels dug into the dirt, and his whole body twisted around like a pretzel. He swung hard.

The baseball rocketed up into the air. It flew over the shortstop's head and into left field. Then it dropped onto an overhang just below the train. Home run!

Bixby jogged around the bases. *WOOOO-WOOOO!* The train whistle echoed through the park. Houston was ahead, three to zero.

Mike and Kate leapt to their feet and

cheered. "Wow!" Mike shouted. "Did you see that? He nailed it! Where did it go?"

"It fell by the gas pump." Mr. Ryan pointed to the overhang above the left-field wall. "See that porch? There's a big gas pump on it. Houston is a major oil town. The pump records the total number of home runs the Astros have hit since the stadium was built. I guess they'll have to add another run to it!"

When everyone sat down, Mr. Hopkins said, "The numbers on the gas pump remind me of something. How about a riddle?"

"Yes!" Kate poked Mike in the chest. "Let's see who's faster today!"

Mike swatted at her hand. "I'm ready to hit a fastball over the gas pump," he said. "Fire away, Uncle Steve."

Mr. Hopkins stroked his chin. "A fastball. That's a good idea," he said.

Mike leaned forward in his seat.

"What's something that only the Astros and two other teams have that is the same, but different?" Mr. Hopkins asked.

Kate twirled her ponytail and looked up at the Houston skyline. Mike tapped his fingers on the arm of his chair. "A gas pump?" he blurted out after looking at the outfield.

"No, not quite, Mike. Think more about fastballs. Not home runs," Mr. Hopkins told him. "Here's a hint. You can see the answer from here."

"Ooh," Kate said. She studied the park. "Fastballs. Fastballs. Pitching. Pitchers . . . ," she muttered to herself.

Mike jumped up to scan the field. He didn't want to let Kate win. "It's, um—"

"Nolan Ryan!" Kate said. She slapped her hand on her armrest. "Nolan Ryan's number is right up there!" She pointed to a giant baseball with the number thirty-four on it above the scoreboard.

"That's right, Kate," her dad said. "Good job! Nolan Ryan was a famous fastball pitcher. Three different teams have retired his number. But two of them retired the number thirty-four, and one retired the number thirty. So they're the same, but different."

Kate flexed her muscles at Mike. "Looks like *I* hit that one over the gas pump."

"Maybe, but I let you win," Mike said with a wave of his hand. "How about another riddle, Uncle Steve?"

"Nice try, Mike," Mr. Hopkins laughed. "Let's watch the game for now."

Two more batters reached base, but the Rockies made a double play and struck the next batter out. The inning was over.

"Dad, can we go see if Commander Rice is here?" Kate asked.

"Sure," Mr. Hopkins said. "Just don't leave the ballpark. I'll keep an eye on the game for you."

Kate and Mike jogged up the steps and down a wide hallway. To the left of the main entrance was a long table. Behind it hung a banner that read COMMANDER NICHOLAS RICE. On the table in front of an empty chair lay a stack of pictures of Commander Rice in a blue flight suit. A security guard stood behind the other end of the table. He was busy talking into a walkie-talkie.

Kate leafed through the photos. None were signed. "Where's Commander Rice?" she asked Mike. "I thought he'd be signing autographs by now."

"Maybe he's still missing," Mike said. He

wiggled his fingers in front of Kate's face and dropped his voice. "Or maybe he's lost in space."

Kate rolled her eyes. "Real funny," she said. "We should wait for him."

Mike took out his baseball and started tossing it. Then an exhibit on the other side of the doorway caught his eye. It showed the history of Houston's Union Station. Years ago, Union Station was Houston's biggest train station. Now it was the main entrance to the Astros' ballpark. Rows of black-and-white pictures of steam trains, passenger cars, and the old train station hung in the display.

At the end of the display, Mike spotted a clear plastic box about the size of a garbage can. It was filled with black chunks of coal.

"Hey, come here," Mike called out to Kate. "It's a box full of coal. The steam trains like the one on the outfield wall used to run on it.

You can reach in and touch the coal pieces!"

Mike dipped his hand through a round opening at the top of the box. The shiny black chunks of coal were smooth. But some had jagged edges. "Try it," he said.

Kate stuck her hand in. "Feels cold," she said. "But we came down here to see Commander Rice, not a train display. Let's ask that security guard if he knows anything."

Mike followed Kate over to the guard behind the table. He had just put down his walkie-talkie. The name tag on his shirt read LUIS.

"Excuse me," Kate said. "We're friends of Commander Rice. Do you know when he's coming?"

Luis shook his head. "He was upstairs about an hour ago for a party," he said. He pointed to a nearby stairway. "But Commander Rice didn't show up for the first pitch like he was supposed to. They had to start the game without him. We've been looking but haven't found him yet."

"Thanks," Kate said. "We'll check back later."

Kate and Mike took the stairway up to the next level. It wasn't very busy. Mike could see a few fans farther down the hallway.

Mike nodded to a sign on the door in front of them. It read COMMANDER RICE PARTY. "Maybe someone in there knows what happened to him." He pulled the door open and stepped inside.

Kate slipped in, too. She expected the room to be full of businesspeople. But it was empty, except for a few round tables. Half-filled cups and plates of leftovers sat on the tables around the room.

"I guess the party's over," Mike said.

"Everyone must have gone to their seats when the game started."

"I'm not sure we should be here," Kate said. She glanced over her shoulder to the door. "What if someone finds us?"

Mike shrugged. "We'll just tell them exactly what we're doing. We're looking for Commander Rice. No one said to keep out."

For the next five minutes, Kate and Mike searched the room. All they found were a few business cards and some Astros stickers.

"There's no sign of Commander Rice," Mike said. Just then, the crowd roared. There must have been a big play. "Let's go. We're missing the game!"

Mike and Kate left the party room. Mike was halfway down the stairs when he heard Kate call him.

"Mike! Stop!" Kate said.

Mike turned around. Kate stood at the top of the stairs. Her head was tilted like she was listening for something.

"Why?" Mike asked. "What—"

Kate put her finger up to her lips. "Shh . . . ,"

she said. She pointed at a door marked EMPLOYEES ONLY. "I hear something."

Kate put her ear against the door. Her eyes grew wide. "Something is scratching on the other side!"

Knock, Knock

Mike bounded up the steps. When he reached Kate, he leaned over and pressed his ear against the door, too. Silence. But then they both heard it. A few seconds of soft scratching, like sandpaper on a piece of wood.

Mike straightened up. "It sounds like mice," he said.

"No," Kate said. "Someone's there. I heard tapping. Like a signal."

Kate rapped the door hard three times with her knuckles. *KNOCK, KNOCK, KNOCK.*

She motioned for Mike to lean against the door again. But there was no response.

Mike shook his head. "See, it's probably just a mouse." He turned to go. Kate stepped back to study the wall.

KNOCK, KNOCK, KNOCK.

Mike whirled around. "That's no mouse!"

Mike twisted the door handle and pulled. The door moved slightly, but then stuck fast. Kate reached over. She helped Mike give it another tug. The door sprang open. Someone was huddled on the floor behind it.

It was Commander Rice!

He wore a blue zip-up flight suit, and his hands and feet were bound with tape. A strip of cloth was tied around his head. It covered his mouth. Mike knelt down and untied it. When it fell away, Commander Rice gasped for air.

"Thank you!" he said as Kate worked on
the tape around his feet and hands. The commander winced.

"Are you okay?" Kate asked.

"I think so," Commander Rice replied. "Someone knocked me out." He touched the back of his head. "Wow. I didn't see that coming! Did I miss the first pitch?"

Kate looked at her phone. "It's about eight o'clock," she said. "You missed the start of the game. That's why we came looking for you. What happened?"

Commander Rice stood up and rubbed the marks on his wrists. He stretched for a moment while he was thinking. "I'm not sure. I was at the party. It was for local businesspeople, including some from the tour this morning, like Sam and Tex and Manuel." He ran his fingers through his blond hair. "I left about twenty minutes before the game to get ready."

"Someone must have been watching you and waiting for you to leave!" Kate said.

"I didn't see anyone suspicious," Commander Rice said. "They must have been waiting for me in the hall." He scanned the hallway as he tried to remember what happened.

Mike studied the hallway, too. He pulled out his baseball and tried to roll it from one hand to the other, but the ball dropped onto the floor. Mike scrambled to pick it up before it rolled down the stairs.

Commander Rice snapped his fingers. "That's it. I saw a ten-dollar bill right there." He pointed to the floor in front of the door, where Mike's ball had bounced. "I bent down to pick it up, and someone put something over my face. It smelled a little like straw. They dragged me into this room and knocked me out."

Commander Rice's hand went to the back of his head again. "It still hurts. I faded in and out for a while, but I remember hearing deep voices," he said. "The next thing I knew, I woke up all tied up. I started trying to get the ropes off. Then I heard you knocking."

He frowned, trying to remember more. "They said something about meeting at a gas station near the hill, deep in the heart of Texas," Commander Rice said. He shook his head to clear it.

"I'll bet they were talking about their hide-out!" Mike said.

"Houston's near the bottom of the state," Kate said. "If they're meeting in the heart of Texas, it's probably far away from here. There's a lot of space in Texas."

Commander Rice gasped. His face went pale. "Space!" He looked around the room wildly. "It's gone!" he said.

"What's gone?" Mike asked.

"My briefcase," Commander Rice said. He pulled the pockets of his flight suit inside out. They were empty except for some blue fuzz.

"The key is missing, too!" he said. "It was in my pocket."

Mike snorted. "At least it was only work stuff," he said. "I wouldn't mind it if someone stole my homework!"

"No, Mike. They didn't steal work papers," Commander Rice said. "They stole the moon rock!"

The Astro Outlaw

"The moon rock is gone?" Kate gasped.

"I had it when I left the party, and it's not here now," Commander Rice said. "That must be why they mugged me. The moon rocks brought back by the Apollo missions are worth a huge amount of money!"

"Like, how much?" Mike asked.

"A lot," Commander Rice said. "Back in 1998, a thief tried to sell a moon rock from *Apollo Seventeen* for five million dollars!"

"Wow," Mike said. "That would buy a lot

of baseball tickets! Whoever stole your moon rock must be a real outlaw!"

"You mean an *Astro* Outlaw," Kate said.

Mike laughed. "The Astro Outlaw. I like it! Let's search the room. Maybe the Astro Outlaw left some clues!"

The room was only about ten feet long and ten feet wide. The floor was dark gray concrete, and the walls were made of cinder block. A light hung from the ceiling. On the far wall was a second door. A sign on it read TRACKS. EMPLOYEES ONLY.

Mike elbowed Kate in the ribs. "Look, maybe the Outlaw left some tracks!" he said.

Kate groaned at Mike's bad joke. But Commander Rice smiled for the first time since Kate and Mike had found him. He cracked the door open a few inches. Right away, the sound of the baseball game grew louder. He pulled the door open completely.

"The thieves didn't leave *these* tracks, Mike," Kate said. In front of them stretched the railroad tracks for the stadium's train. They could see the train engine's big red cow-catcher, large light, and black smokestack. To their right were the outfield and third base. A walkway ran next to the train tracks.

"This must be how the engineer gets to the train," Mike said. "Cool!"

"Well, the Outlaw wouldn't have hidden the moon rock out here," Commander Rice said. "I bet whoever stole the rock has already taken it out of the stadium. Or he's hidden it somewhere."

Just as Commander Rice was closing the door, Mike called, "Wait!" He pointed to the tracks. Something black lay between the rails about ten feet away. "What's that?" he asked.

"My briefcase!" Commander Rice said. He picked it up. The black case had a blue and red NASA sticker on the side. "It's unlocked!"

Commander Rice's hands shook as he popped open the cover. The briefcase was fitted with gray foam inside. In the middle was a hollow space for the moon rock. The commander's shoulders slumped. "Empty," he said.

"Hey, that's the right size for a baseball," Mike said. He slipped his baseball into the hole in the case's gray foam. It fit perfectly. "But I guess that moon rock is more valuable than my baseball." He took the baseball back.

Commander Rice snapped his briefcase closed and headed for the hallway. "I have to go report this," he said. Kate followed him out.

As Mike turned to go, something on the ground by the door to the tracks caught his eye. "What's that?" he said. He picked up the top half of a green feather. "It's broken right in the middle."

"Why didn't we see that before?" Kate asked.

Commander Rice studied the feather. Then he looked at the door. "I'll bet it was caught in the door," he said.

"That means it must have fallen out when we opened the door," Kate said. "It might have come from whoever took your briefcase!"

"Maybe a parrot stole the moon rock," Mike said with a grin. "They're green."

Commander Rice smiled and held up the feather. "I don't think a parrot could have carried away the moon rock, Mike. Plus, if you look at its edge you can tell it was dyed green. It used to be gray."

Kate stared at the broken feather. "That means the Astro Outlaw has the other half.

It's like a jigsaw puzzle!" Kate loved solving puzzles.

Commander Rice nodded. He slipped the feather into his pocket. "I don't know how we'll find him," he said, shutting the door to the tracks. He looked around the small room one more time.

"Why don't you kids watch the game for a while?" he said. "After I go to security, I'll be downstairs to sign autographs. Come back during the seventh-inning stretch."

Mike nodded. "Don't forget to tell them about the Astro Outlaw and his gas station deep in the heart of Texas!"

Hot, Hot, Hot

By the time Kate and Mike returned to their seats in the fifth inning, the Colorado Rockies were ahead by one run.

"*Hola,* Kate! *Hola,* Mike!" Mr. Hopkins said. He spoke Spanish and was helping Kate learn it as well. Mr. Hopkins put down his program. "Did you find Commander Rice?" he asked.

"Yes! You won't believe it. He'd been knocked out cold!" Mike blurted out. "And someone stole the moon rock!"

Kate's dad and Mr. Ryan looked shocked.

"Is he okay?" Mr. Ryan asked.

"He's got a bump on his head, but he seems fine," Kate said. She explained how they had found the astronaut tied up. She also told them about how Mike had found the green feather.

"Wow. That's some story!" Mr. Hopkins said, shaking his head.

"I'll say," Mr. Ryan said. He mopped his brow and brushed back his frizzy black hair. "Maybe I should go check on things." He stood up to leave. "I'll meet you after the game, near the entrance."

Mike looked at the scoreboard above the right-field seats. "I can't believe the Rockies are winning. Tommy Thompson's fastball is close to ninety-eight miles per hour! How are the Rockies getting hits off him?"

"He's having a bad day," Kate's dad said. "The Astros—"

In the background, the loudspeaker boomed to life. "And now, it's time for the Houston Hot Sauce Race!" A gate opened in the right outfield corner, and three figures popped out. They were dressed as tall, thin packets of hot sauce. The first one was bright red. The second was yellow. And the last one was orange. Only their arms and legs stuck out of the costumes.

"Pick which hot sauce will win today's race!" the announcer went on. "Will it be Mild, Medium, or Hot?"

Mike's eyes lit up. "Oh boy! I think Hot will win." He had his eyes on the bright red hot-sauce packet.

"I'm picking Mild," Kate said. "I like yellow. That leaves you with Medium, Dad."

When the announcer shouted "Go!" the human hot sauces bumbled down the dirt

warning track. Medium led the race most of
the way. But as they rounded home, Mild took
the lead. Mild was steps away from the line
when Hot shot up from behind and bumped
him aside. Hot broke through the blue crepe-
paper finish line first!

"Hot has won again!" boomed the loud-speaker. "I guess we like things fiery here in Houston."

"Told you so!" Mike said. He waved his index finger in the air like a number one sign. He loved competing against Kate. "I win . . . *again,*" he said, although he knew he didn't win as often as he liked.

Kate grabbed Mike's finger. "Yeah, but only because your hot sauce pushed mine out of the way," she said. "Don't worry, Mike. They're just hot-sauce packets, so they'll all be squeezed in the end!"

Mike tried to pull his finger away but couldn't. He didn't like to admit it, but when she wanted to be, Kate was pretty strong. "I was just, um, stretching my fingers!" he said.

Kate gave Mike's finger one last tight squeeze and let go.

"Well, speaking of hot sauce," Mike said, "how about we get some? Like on a hot dog or some fries?"

"Great idea," Kate said, jumping up. "We can race to see who's faster!"

"You don't want to leave now," Mr. Hopkins said. "Adam Bixby is batting."

Mike and Kate settled back in their seats as Bixby strode to the plate. He leaned over, touched home plate with his pinkie, and said a prayer. Then he took two slow practice swings and waited for the pitcher. The tip of the bat made small circles in the air behind his shoulder. It looked like a bee getting ready to sting.

The pitcher wound up and flung a fastball inside. Bixby's bat sliced down across the plate. STRIKE ONE!

The catcher threw the ball back, and Bixby returned to his batting stance. The tip of the bat buzzed in circles behind his head. Once more, the pitcher unloaded. He launched a slider toward home plate. But instead of dropping down, the ball hung in the strike zone. Again the bat flashed across the plate. Bixby's wrists snapped the bat forward.

POW!

He connected. The ball zoomed high over second base. Bixby dropped the bat, put his head down, and raced to first. The Rockies' center fielder sprinted back to the wall. He passed the dirt warning track and sped up a small grassy hill in front of the outfield wall. But the ball dropped just over the fence.

Another home run for Bixby! Now the game was tied!

"What a hit!" Mike exclaimed over the noise of the train whistle and the cheers. "But why is there a hill in center field, Uncle Steve?

Is that legal? I've never seen a baseball field with hills!"

Kate's dad smiled. "It's called Tal's Hill," he said when the noise died down. "A lot of old-fashioned ballparks used to have hills or other uneven areas in the outfield. The Astros thought it would be fun to have one here. So they built the hill. They also added a flagpole near the top of the hill. Outfielders have to watch out for that!"

The inning ended with a pop fly. The center fielder caught it for an easy out.

"Ready for that hot dog now, Mike?" Kate asked. "Dad, do you want anything?"

Mr. Hopkins shook his head. "No thanks," he said as he handed them some money. "I'm going to buy some of those Kick'n Hot Nachos later. Have fun!"

Food and drink stands lined the main hall.

Texas favorites like nachos, chili, and fajitas sat side by side with hand-carved smoked turkey sandwiches, foot-long hot dogs, snow cones, and cotton candy. Mike and Kate threaded their way from one stand to another, between fans in cowboy boots and hats. It was hard to decide!

Kate finally settled on a taco. *"Un taco con queso, por favor,"* she said in Spanish to the woman behind the counter.

"Cinco dólares," the woman replied.

"I like that so many people speak Spanish in Texas!" Kate said. She tasted the taco with cheese and offered a bite to Mike. He chomped down on it as they went to wait in line for some kettle corn.

"Hey, Mike," Kate said. "Check out the hat on that man over there." She pointed to a man at the water fountain. He wore blue jeans,

54

an Astros shirt, and a tan cowboy hat. The
hat had a black band around it. There was a
bright red feather stuck in the band.

"A feather!" Mike said. "That looks like the one we found, except it's red."

"Exactly," Kate said. "Now look at the other fans with cowboy hats."

Mike scanned the crowd. Many of the cowboy hats had some type of small feather in the band. Most were bright shades of red, blue, green, yellow, or orange.

Mike couldn't believe his eyes. "Feathers— they're everywhere!"

"I'll bet the one you found came from the Outlaw's cowboy hat!" Kate said. She snapped her fingers. "And you know what else? Remember how Commander Rice said he smelled straw?"

Mike nodded.

"Some cowboy hats are made of felt or wool. But others are made of straw," Kate said. "Maybe the Outlaw put a cowboy hat over Commander Rice's face! All we have to do is find someone with a broken green feather in their hat!"

Mike groaned. "But, Kate, almost *everyone* here is wearing a cowboy hat."

"Yeah," Kate agreed with a sigh. "Still, let's keep our eyes open, just in case."

Mike paid for his food, and they went to their seats. The sixth inning had just started. While Mike popped bits of kettle corn into his mouth and took swigs of red PowerPunch, Kate wolfed down her taco. Neither team scored in the sixth, and soon the Rockies were up for the top of the seventh inning. The first Rockies batter hit a double. But the Astros made three quick outs and hustled off the field. It was time for the seventh-inning stretch.

Fans stood up as the sounds of organ

music filled the stadium. The grounds crew neatened up the infield.

"Take me out to the ball game. Take me out with the crowd. . . ."

Kate jumped up. "We'll see you later, Dad," she said. "Mike and I are going to see how Commander Rice is doing. Come on, Mike." She gave Mike's T-shirt a tug. "Let's go get an astronaut's autograph!"

Deep in the Heart
of Texas

The main hallway was busy with people. "I'm glad we ate earlier," Mike said. "Check out those lines."

He and Kate passed souvenir stands with racks of baseballs, red Astros hats, key chains, and packs of baseball cards.

"Hey, before we see Commander Rice, can we take a look at the gas pump?" Mike asked. "I want to see how many home runs the Astros have hit."

"Okay," Kate said. "He's probably busy during the seventh-inning stretch anyway."

The sounds of the crowd singing along with the organ music drifted through the stadium.

"It's one, two, three strikes, you're out, at the old ball gaaaaaaaame. . . ."

Up ahead, the hallway widened. To the left were the main entrance and the table where Commander Rice sat, signing autographs. To the right was the train display. From there, a hallway ran along the outfield.

In the background, "Take Me Out to the Ball Game" changed into another song. Kate stopped and listened. It wasn't the baseball anthem anymore, but she'd heard the melody before. Everyone knew the words.

Bum-bum-bummmm. Bum-bum-bummmm. "The stars at night are big and bright." CLAP-CLAP-CLAP-CLAP.

Then it hit her. She knew the name of the song!

"Mike!" Kate called out. "Wait up!"

Mike was already down the hall at the gas pump. Kate sprinted to catch up with him. When she did, he was circling the largest gas pump that Kate had ever seen. The pump was about thirteen feet tall and painted bright white. The words HOME RUN PUMP were written in red on the sides. Red numbers counted up the home run total.

"It's huge!" he said. "Usually gas pumps show how many gallons of gas are sold. But this one shows how many home runs the Astros hit since they built this park! Pretty cool!"

"I know something even cooler," Kate said. She grabbed his arm and pulled him to the overhang. "Listen! Listen to the song that's playing!"

"The prairie sky is wide and high"—CLAP-CLAP-CLAP-CLAP—*"deep in the heart of Texas."*

Mike had a puzzled look on his face. "So? They play both 'Take Me Out to the Ball Game' and 'Deep in the Heart of Texas' for the seventh-inning stretch."

"Don't you see?" Kate said to Mike. "It's what Commander Rice heard the thieves saying!"

Mike's frown vanished. "They said they were meeting at a gas station near the hill, deep in the heart of Texas!" he said.

"Exactly," Kate whispered. She nodded at the gas pump. "They're meeting at a gas station." She turned Mike around so he was facing the flagpole in the outfield. "By a hill." She pointed to Tal's Hill, the grassy slope in the outfield. "Get it?"

"So the hill isn't deep in the middle of Texas after all," Mike said.

"No," Kate said. "It's right here. That wasn't *where* they were meeting. It was *when* they were meeting."

Mike's eyes grew wide. "That means they might be meeting right now, right here!"

Kate nodded. "Quick! Let's hide somewhere and watch." She dragged Mike to a tall pillar across the hallway. From behind it, they could see everyone near the pump.

The song ended. The Rockies ran out to take the field. The Astros' first batter warmed up on the field. The people near the gas pump didn't look suspicious. Most of them stopped by the railing and looked down at the baseball diamond. A family with three small boys, an old man, and two women walked by. None of them seemed like thieves.

After a few minutes, Mike started to get antsy. "Maybe we missed them," he said. "The game's starting again."

"Let's stay a little while longer," Kate said. Her voice dropped to a whisper. "What about them?"

Kate pointed to a man and a woman next to the gas pump. The woman held a plastic shopping bag. Something heavy sat at the bottom. The man kept checking his watch and glancing toward the main exit.

"Maybe the moon rock is in that bag!" Kate said.

A small boy ran up to them. The woman reached into the bag. She pulled out a bright white baseball and gave it to him. The boy's face lit up, and he hugged the woman. The three walked off together.

"Or maybe not," Mike said. "This is a bust."

"Wait—look at that," Kate said. A business-man holding a leather briefcase stood to the right of the gas pump. He was talking with a shorter man wearing a suit.

"That could be him. He might have the rock in that briefcase," Kate said. "But we've got to see who he's talking to."

Just then, a bunch of teenagers crowded onto the porch near the gas pump. The men looked over their shoulders at them and shifted closer to where Mike and Kate were hiding. As they did, a third person came into view. He wore a black straw cowboy hat, jeans, a jacket, and shiny black boots.

"Shoot," Mike said. "That's just Tex Ray-burn from Fat Hats."

Kate clutched his arm. "Holy Toledo!" she gasped.

After a moment, Mike spotted what Kate

was talking about. His jaw dropped open.

Tucked into Tex's hatband were three green feathers. The one in the middle was broken neatly in half!

Round Up!

Mike caught his breath. "Tex Rayburn is the thief?" he asked. "But he's so nice!"

"It all fits together," Kate said. She ticked off the facts. "He knew about the moon rock. He was at the party with Commander Rice. And the feather we found matches the one on his hat! I like him, too, but I'm sure he's the Astro Outlaw!"

Over by the gas pump, Tex and his partner were still talking to the businessman. The man flipped the briefcase open for a second.

Tex smiled. Then Tex held open the pocket of his jacket to show the man something. The man nodded.

"I'll bet he's got the moon rock in his jacket pocket!" Kate said. "But what's in the briefcase?"

"Money," Mike said. "Didn't you see the way Tex smiled when the man opened it? It's probably full of money to pay for the moon rock!"

"We've got to stop them," Kate said. "There's no time to lose!"

Blending in with the people passing by, Mike and Kate raced down the corridor. Near the main entrance, they spied Commander Rice signing autographs. Kate and Mike ran to the head of the line. Kate cut in front of a tall man wearing a red and gold Astros jersey.

Commander Rice looked surprised to see them. He was just about to say something when the tall man spoke up.

"Hey, the end of the line is back there, darlin'," the man said. He pointed behind him. "Y'all need to wait your turn."

"I'm sorry," Kate said. "But it's an emergency!" She looked Commander Rice in the eyes. "We've found the moon rock! You've got to come to the gas pump right now. Before they get away!"

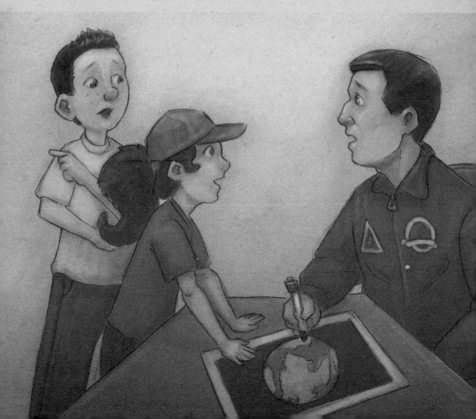

Commander Rice slid back his chair. "I'll be right back," he said to the line of people waiting for autographs. He placed his left hand on the table and jumped over it in one move. Then he called to Luis, the security guard, "Can you radio for help at the gas pump?"

Luis nodded and picked up his walkie-talkie.

As they ran down the hallway, Kate told Commander Rice about the meeting at the pump.

When they were almost there, Kate spied two policemen walking toward them from the other end of the hallway. Over near the gas pump, Tex was shaking hands with the man holding the briefcase. A few fans nearby were leaning over the railing, watching the game.

Tex started to pull something out of his jacket pocket. But then he spied the policemen coming from the other direction. He instantly turned around, took off his hat, and mopped his brow. Without saying a word to his partner, Tex put his hat on and headed for the exit at a fast pace.

Tex walked right past Mike, Kate, and Commander Rice. When he passed, Commander Rice said, "Mr. Rayburn! Stop! We need to ask you a few questions!"

Tex took off running.

"He's headed for the exit!" Commander Rice shouted to the police officers. "Stop him!"

Fans moved out of the way as Tex ran down the hall. The two policemen followed closely. The sound of running feet echoed on the tiled floor.

Just as Tex was about to reach the main entrance, he slipped and crashed into the train display. His body slammed against the big box of coal, and he spun off into the center of the hallway. Tex twirled around twice. He lost

his balance and then fell to the floor. His head knocked against the hard tile with a *thud*.

Seconds later, the police reached Tex. He was sprawled on the ground. A crowd of people gathered around them.

"He's hurt!" Kate said.

"Nah, I'll bet he's just faking it," Mike said.

The police held everyone back. Then Tex moved.

"See? He's okay," Mike said.

With the help of the police, Tex sat up, holding the side of his head. Two paramedics arrived. They put Tex on a stretcher and carried him away. The policemen and Commander Rice led the man with the briefcase and Tex's partner into a nearby office. Soon after, the crowd drifted off. Kate texted her father to let him know where they were. Just as Mike and Kate were about to go back to their seats, they heard their names.

"Kate, Mike!" Commander Rice called out. He was standing near the train display that Tex had crashed into. "You were right about the feather!"

He had Tex's hat in his hand. When Kate and Mike made it over to him, Commander Rice took an envelope from his pocket. He opened it and pulled out the half of the green feather that Kate and Mike had found in the room upstairs. He held it up against the broken green feather on the hat. It matched perfectly!

Kate gave Mike a high five. "I knew it!" she said. "He must have knocked you out. He put you in the room and was trying to sell the moon rock!"

"I'm afraid so," Commander Rice said. "Sometimes even nice people turn out to be trouble."

A look of concern passed over Kate's face. "What's going to happen?" she asked. "Is Tex okay?"

"He's fine. It's just a bump on the head," said Commander Rice. "We've already searched all three men. None of them had the moon rock. They said they didn't even know it was missing. Yes, the briefcase was loaded with money. But the man said it was for work."

"Tex sure looked guilty when he started running," Mike said. "He was hightailing it out of here!"

Commander Rice frowned. "Tex claimed

he was just in a hurry to get back to his hat store. He said he didn't hear me telling him to stop. If he did steal the moon rock, he sure didn't have it when he ran down the hallway!"

"What are you going to do?" Mike asked.

"I'm going back to the security office to see if I can help," Commander Rice said. "They're going to question Tex. His story is fishy. But so far they can't prove he had the moon rock."

"Is there any way we can help?" Kate asked. She held her thumb and index finger about an inch apart. "It feels like we were *this* close to finding the moon rock!"

"I know," Commander Rice said. "But there's nothing else for you to do. Tex is in custody. Security is going to check everyone going out to make sure they don't have the rock with them. Go to your seats, and then stop by my table after the game. I'll give you an update."

As Commander Rice turned to go, four security officers passed by. They spread out next to the exit doors and started checking the bags of people leaving.

Commander Rice shook his head sadly. "That moon rock is priceless. I hope they find it before it's gone forever!"

The Hidden-Ball Trick

Kate paced back and forth.

"Kate, Commander Rice said we should go back to our seats," Mike said. He leaned against Commander Rice's empty table near the stadium entrance. "They caught Tex. The security people are watching the doors. Maybe we should go watch the game."

Kate stopped and drummed her fingers on the table. "It feels like we're missing something," she said. "*We* know that Tex must have had the moon rock in his pocket when he was at the gas pump. If he doesn't have it now, it *has* to be here somewhere! I'm not ready to give up."

Kate pushed away from the table. She headed back down the hallway to the gas pump. Mike shook his head and raced to catch up.

When they reached the gas pump, Kate started searching right away. But Mike wandered over to one of the railings overlooking the field. He wanted to check the score.

It was the top of the ninth inning. The Astros were ahead by one run, but the Rockies had just hit a double. Their player had barely missed being thrown out at second. A home run would put them ahead.

Mike leaned forward. He spun his baseball around in his hands. This was a key point in the game. The players knew it, too.

The second baseman threw the ball back to the pitcher. As he did, the catcher headed out for a conference. The pitcher met him at the grass on the side of the mound. The infielders jogged in as well. After talking for a few moments, the players returned to their positions.

On the edge of the grass, the pitcher leaned down to tie his shoe. When he finished, he turned to take the mound. The runner on second stepped off the base to take a lead. As soon as he did, the second baseman reached over and tagged him. Then the second baseman opened his glove. The ball was hidden inside! He had taken it during the meeting at the mound!

The umpire yanked his hand back and yelled, "YOU'RE OUT!"

The runner looked confused. He threw up

his hands. The Rockies' manager marched out onto the field.

"Kate! You've got to see this," Mike said.

"What?" Kate asked. She stepped up to the railing beside Mike.

"The Astros' second baseman just pulled off the hidden-ball trick!" Mike said.

"The hidden-ball trick?" she repeated. "What's that?"

Mike pointed to the jumbo TV on the scoreboard. It showed the play in slow motion. "That's when you've got a runner on base. You pretend to give the ball back to the pitcher, but don't," he said. "The ball is still in play as long as the pitcher doesn't step on the pitching rubber. Then, when the runner leaves the base, he's tagged out! That's soooo tricky!"

Kate laughed. "That's great! The runner fell for it?"

"Yup!" Mike said. "I've read about it, but I've never seen it in a major-league game before!"

The manager of the Rockies tried to argue with the umpire that the runner was safe. But the umpire shook his head, and the manager headed back to the dugout. The runner was out. Now the Astros needed only one more out to win.

Mike kept watching the game, but Kate turned away. She frowned at the gas pump. "Mike, come here," she said. Mike took one more look at the game, then jogged over to Kate.

She put herself near the gas pump where Tex had stood. "I know that Tex had that moon rock in his pocket when we were watching him," she said. Kate pointed to the main entrance. "But he didn't have it when they searched him down there. What happened to it?"

Mike shrugged. "I don't know," he said. He couldn't get his mind off the hidden-ball trick. It worked because everyone thought the pitcher had the ball. But it was really hidden in the fielder's glove.

Then it hit him. "The second baseman!" Mike cried, startling Kate. "The ball was hidden in his glove. What if Tex found a place to hide the moon rock before the police caught him?"

"But how?" Kate asked. "We watched him the whole time."

"I don't know. But the runner didn't think the second baseman had the ball, either," Mike said. "Let's look for hiding places."

They started at the gas pump. But there was no place to hide anything. Its white sides were smooth. Around it on all four sides was a tile floor.

Next, they retraced Tex's path.

"When he saw the police, he left the pump," Kate said. "Then, when Commander Rice called his name, he started running."

Kate bounded down the hallway, taking

big Tex-like steps. She stopped halfway and waited for Mike to catch up.

"He almost made it to the main entrance," Kate said. She pointed to the doors ahead of them. The security guards were still checking the fans who were leaving. Kate looked at the train display to their right. "But he bumped into the display first."

Mike's eyes lit up. He jumped forward and imitated Tex slamming into the display. He careened off into the center of the hallway.

"It knocked him off balance," Kate said. Mike spun around a few times. "And then he fell." Mike slumped to the ground. Kate came up and stood over him. Mike was pretending to be knocked out. "Somehow the rock dis-appeared. Unless . . ."

She noticed a piece of crumpled paper next to Mike's foot.

Kate stepped on it and flattened it against the floor. She shrugged. "Unless he wrapped it up in a sheet of paper and then dropped it, like it was trash. I'll bet that's it! Help me look for a balled-up piece of paper!"

Mike opened his eyes and popped up. "Great idea!" he said, scanning the floor. Plenty of paper littered the floor. Kate and Mike scurried around picking up one piece after another. Each one they opened was empty. Then Mike spotted a large ball of yellow paper by the train display.

As Mike bent down to scoop up the paper, he leaned on the box of coal. He picked up the paper, but like the others, it was empty. Mike tossed it in a nearby trash can. He dipped his hand in the box of coal again. Most of the pieces felt smooth and glassy.

Suddenly, he knew.

"Kate!" he called. "It's not a piece of paper we're looking for! It's a rock!"

Kate looked over at Mike. "I know it's a rock," she said. "How does that help?"

A big grin spread across his face. "It's just like the hidden-ball trick!" he said. "To fool the runner, you hide the ball in a different glove. To fool the police, Tex hid the moon rock with other rocks!"

Mike pulled his hand out of the coal box and held it up for Kate to see. Sitting in his palm was a baseball-size hunk of black moon rock!

Houston, Problem Solved!

"What does Commander Rice want to show us?" Mike asked Kate's dad. Mr. Hopkins had just parked the rental car in an empty parking lot across the street from the Astros' ballpark. Later that afternoon the three were going to the airport. Kate and Mike had a flight to New York, and Mr. Hopkins was returning to Los Angeles.

"He just said to stop by this morning before we left," Kate's dad said. He shielded his eyes and looked for the Union Station entrance. The hot sun shimmered in waves off the blacktop.

The stadium was deserted, but a security guard let them in. He brought them to a room on the upper level. Commander Rice and Mr. Ryan welcomed them.

"We're glad you could come back," Mr. Ryan said, standing up. "We wanted to let you know that Tex has been arrested for the theft of the moon rock. Take a look at this."

Mr. Ryan dimmed the lights and pressed a button on a nearby computer. A short movie was displayed on the large monitor on the wall. The scene showed baseball fans walking near the main entrance.

"This was taken by a security camera. Shortly, you'll see our friend Tex come into the picture," Mr. Ryan said. He pointed to the top of the image with his stubby fingers.

For a few seconds, the video showed only fans walking by. Then Mike, Kate, and Mr. Hopkins could see a commotion near the top of the frame. The video slowed down as Tex ran toward the entrance. People moved out of his way. Before he reached the train display, they saw his hand dart out of his pocket. As he crashed into the box of coal, he dropped a black object into the box. Then he spun off in circles and fell to the floor.

Commander Rice turned the lights back on.

"It's just like we thought!" Mike said. "Tex hid the rock in the box of coal!"

"That's right, Mike," Mr. Ryan said. "He knew he was going to be caught by our guards, so he got rid of the moon rock. He hoped that we couldn't prove anything against him. And, without you two, we wouldn't have. We might not have even bothered looking at the security video, since everyone saw him try to escape."

"What's going to happen to him?" Mr. Hopkins asked.

"Well, when we showed him this tape, Tex confessed," said Mr. Ryan. "His hat store was losing money, and he needed to pay off some loans. He thought he could sell the moon rock."

"What happened to it?" Mike asked.

"I'm glad you asked, Mike," Commander Rice said. "It's back at the Johnson Space Center now, safe in one of our vaults. I guess next time I take it out, I'll have a guard with me."

"That sounds like a good idea," said Mike. "And I have another one. Next time you go up in space, you can take *me* with you! I always wanted to ride a rocket."

Commander Rice laughed. "'Fraid not, Mike. You'll have to figure out a way to ride a rocket on your own," he said.

"Study and work hard, Mike. Then you can become an astronaut like Commander Rice," Mr. Hopkins said with a smile. "Playing big-league baseball isn't your only career option."

"Hmmm-mmm." Mr. Ryan cleared his throat. "Well, actually, I might be able to help you out with that request, Mike. As long as you keep an open mind about the word *rocket*. Let me show you something."

Mr. Ryan led the group back out into the stadium. They walked up the same stairs where Mike and Kate had heard the tapping the day before. Mr. Ryan opened the door at the top, and they all stepped through it.

"So this is where you found Commander Rice," Mr. Hopkins said. "Good work, you two!"

Mr. Ryan flipped the light on. He walked across the room and knocked loudly on the door marked TRACKS. EMPLOYEES ONLY.

"The Astros were so happy that you solved the mystery of the missing moon rock that we wanted to do something special for you," Mr. Ryan said. "That's why I've invited Jimmy to help us. He's what some people, a long time ago, used to call a rocket engineer."

With a squeak, the door opened. Jimmy was on the other side, dressed in blue overalls. He took off his blue-and-white train engineer's hat.

"When trains were first invented, people thought they went as fast as rockets," Jimmy said. "People weren't even sure they'd be able to breathe when the train went above thirty miles an hour. So, we can't help you catch a ride on a real rocket. But we *can* give you two a ride on a nineteenth-century rocket!"

"Cool!" Mike said. He and Kate gave each other a high five.

Jimmy the engineer led Mike and Kate out
to the train. He hoisted them up into the cab
and showed them how to make the train move

forward. Kate gave a big tug on the whistle.
WOOOO-WOOOO! The sound echoed in the
empty stadium. Kate's dad smiled and waved
from the far side of the tracks.

Kate put her arm over her cousin's shoulders. "This has been a great trip," she said to Mike, ticking off the reasons on her fingers. "We got to see the Astros play. We helped find a real moon rock. And now we're getting a train ride. I guess Texas is so big, anything can happen!"

Ballpark Mysteries 4

Dugout Notes
☆ The Astros' ☆ Ballpark

The roof. The Astros had one of the first roofs in the major leagues that could be opened. That's important in Texas, where it can get pretty hot. The roof takes twelve to twenty minutes to open or close. The Astros even made the roof higher in the middle so baseballs wouldn't hit it!

100

The Astrodome. The Astros used to play in a stadium called the Astrodome. It was the first sports stadium with a domed roof. The first major-league game on imitation grass was played there. That's why fake grass is sometimes called Astroturf.

Union Station. One hundred years ago, trains were a big part of Houston's growth. Today, Astros fans are reminded of that when they go to a game. The largest entrance to the Astros' ballpark is Union Station, which once was Houston's main train station.

The train. When the Astros built their new ballpark in 2000, they put a huge old-fashioned train on top of the left-field wall of the stadium. It's made to look like a train from the 1860s. Behind the train is a large coal tender. The train and tender weigh close to 50,000 pounds.

The gas pump. The history of Houston isn't just trains. It's also oil. Discovery of oil near Houston in 1901 kicked off the huge Texas oil boom. Soon, Houston was home to many major oil companies. To honor that history, the Astros installed a large gas pump on an overhang above left field. The gas pump is thirteen feet tall. It has red numbers on it that count the home runs hit by Astros players since the ballpark opened.

Tal's Hill. There aren't many—or any—other major-league ballparks that have a hill in their outfield. But the Astros decided to put a small, wide hill in deep center field because some old ballparks had hills or uneven fields. Tal's Hill rises at a thirty-degree angle. It's so steep that outfielders have to be careful when they're chasing a fly ball!

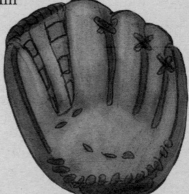

The flagpole. Ballparks aren't supposed to have obstacles in them, either. But the Astros' ballpark has a flagpole in center field, on top of Tal's Hill. The flagpole is also in play. That means if a baseball hits it, the play doesn't stop. The fielder has to get the ball and make the out, if he can.

Crazy uniforms. In the 1970s, the Astros were known for their uniforms. They had bright red, orange, and yellow stripes across the front and on the sleeves. They were very different from other teams' uniforms. But the uniforms looked good on color television, which was new back then. Now the Astros only use the old colorful uniforms for special games.

Nolan Ryan. Nolan Ryan was a hard-throwing right-handed pitcher. His pitches often clocked in at over 100 miles per hour. During his career, he threw seven no-hitters, making him the all-time leader. While playing for the Houston Astros from 1980 to 1988, he threw his fifth no-hitter.  Three teams (the California Angels, the Texas Rangers, and the Houston Astros) retired his number, and he's now in the Baseball Hall of Fame.